Twelve Troubled Jurors

By

Tony Drury

Published by City Fiction

Copyright © 2017 Tony Drury

The right of Tony Drury to be identified as the author of this work has been asserted by him in accordance with the Copyright, Designs and Patents Act 1988

All rights reserved.

This is a work of fiction. Names, characters, businesses, places, events and incidents are either the products of the author's imagination or used in a fictitious manner. Any resemblance to actual persons, living or dead, or actual events is purely coincidental.

No part of this publication may be reproduced, stored in a retrieval system or transmitted in any form or by any means including photocopying, electronic, recording or otherwise, without the prior written permission of the rights holder, application for which must be made through the publisher.

ISBN: 978-1-910040-14-0

My immeasurable thanks must go to Oliver Richbell for his support, guidance and encouragement during the writing of this novella.

TWELVE TROUBLED JURORS

The rather drab jury room at Nailton Crown Court, on the north-west boundary of Greater London, contained two unisex toilets.

Barely visible, through the dirt-encrusted, secured window, was the slow-moving traffic as drivers struggled to breach the road works and reach the relative space of the M40 motorway leading to Oxford and the Midlands. Standing and, in three cases, relaxing, round a long, dull table, were seven men and five women.

The judge, sitting in the case of Geoffrey Maitland-Smith, had directed them, a few minutes earlier, to arrive at a unanimous decision.

The jury officer, a sour-faced man of some fifty years old, was finishing locking away the jurors' mobile phones and laptops, despite their reluctance to part with their only means of communicating with the outside world. One individual in particular created a fuss, but the jury officer had heard it all before.

It was impossible, accurately, to gauge his accent as he rarely spoke and, when he did, it was with an uncaring mutter. There was, perhaps, a hint of a northern twang as he pointed out the flasks of hot water and freeze-dried coffee sachets in the corner of the room, and the jugs of water and plastic cups in the centre of the table.

Then, with a ballroom-esque turn, so that his faded black gown billowed up behind him, he pointed to a sign on the wall by the exit that read 'Press Buzzer for the Jury Officer'. He followed this with a chuntering of words that inaudibly resembled something like "evacuation in the case of any emergency". He closed the door behind him and the click of the lock resonated to the group left inside.

It was 10.22am on Friday morning.

The trial of Geoffrey Maitland-Smith had started on the previous Tuesday which, for five members of the jury, was the seventh of the ten days minimum period they were required to attend court. Several others had been called for selection on previous occasions, and then rejected, leaving them to return to the waiting room. Two of the group had completed shorter trials but were required to stay on because of the ten days' attendance requirement. Within the gathering now assembled in the jury room there were two women who were becoming acquainted. Several of the men had shared a few basic pleasantries over the latest football results, including one who was an avid Arsenal supporter. Another man wanted to talk about politics.

The trial had been procedural and, at times, tense. The judge, as suggested by his inability to sit still, gave the impression he was suffering from haemorrhoids. The defendant had maintained a superior sneer throughout the process except when he was bestowing overt beams of adulation on his defence counsel. She was Amanda Buckingham QC and she maintained a professional poise and, outwardly, ignored her client's admiration.

"Out of here for the afternoon!" said a red-faced,

older man. He coughed rather abruptly and produced an oversized handkerchief which he seemed to attempt to swallow. "It's Friday. He's clearly innocent so let's just get on with it." He spluttered and, after taking a gulp of stale air, continued by proposing that, "We can then go home for the weekend."

A young, tired-looking woman, who was perhaps four months pregnant, suggested that they needed to appoint a foreman.

Yvonne Arrowsmith had deliberately positioned herself at one end of the table and curtly announced that she would be undertaking the role. Several of the male members glanced at each other with cautious surprise. The twelve jurors had been together for four days and, naturally, one or two unspoken alliances had developed. With the exception of Nathan Hercroil, a mixed-race train driver, there was a degree of unease about her personality. He had struggled to understand the events of the past week and was more interested in Yvonne's physical appearance.

"Please all sit down," continued Ms Arrowsmith. There then ensued the inevitable game of musical chairs, with some shuffling their seats to create more room for themselves. Several others dived straight into helping themselves to a coffee.

"It's rather straightforward," continued Yvonne, as she enjoyed her moment of assumed authority. "The judge has said he wants a unanimous verdict and that means all twelve of us must agree."

"What if we can't?" asked David Williams. He had taken out a plastic take-away pot, from which he was extracting what appeared to be a sausage sandwich. Several of the women jurors had noticed that, on each day, he brought his breakfast with him. In fact, this was his daily routine and he had decided that there was no need for jury service to change his habits. He liked a sausage sandwich around mid-morning and, as he began eating with noisy relish, several jurors looked away. He had told no-one during the last ten days that he was a suspended school teacher awaiting the preliminary findings of an enquiry into accusations of impropriety made by a pupil. He had thought that the meeting, chaired by his head teacher, with the girl's property developer father, had been a farce – but the concerns he had on the outcome did not seem to be affecting his appetite.

Several others had also brought in food. For the rest, the menu offered by the jury officer was as insipid as their surroundings and the associated costs were, for some, simply unrealistic. Only four jurors selected their lunch from the list shown to them.

"Just listen to me," Yvonne declared, as she banged her fist on the table. "We'll go round the table and have a vote." She looked to her left. "You start," she barked. With little or no pause for reflection, the count began. "Not guilty; not guilty," and again until nine individuals had spoken and repeated the 'not guilty' vote. The tenth juror spoke quietly.

"Guilty," she said.

Yvonne looked to her right.

"Not guilty," said the red-faced older man. He seemed to experience another coughing fit and held his handkerchief to his face. Several jurors looked away as he made an elaborate meal of pinching his nose and spluttering at the same time. He was a big man with a crimson complexion and silvery-grey hair. Perhaps, come December, he'd play the role of Santa Claus if his cough had cleared up by then. But it was not his features, or his ostentatious attitude towards the handkerchief, that disturbed several of his fellow jurors. It was the size of it that made other members blink with wonderment.

"Well, that's that," Yvonne pronounced. "I say "not guilty" and therefore he's innocent. Let's ring for the man in the robe."

"But I said "guilty," came a timid, mouse-like voice to Yvonne's right.

"SHUT UP," she snapped back. "You're out of your depth. All you've talked about for the last week are your bloody children. Just say "not guilty" and we can get on with our lives." As the harshness of Yvonne's outburst echoed round the cramped room she continued, after catching her breath, "I know you don't have a job but I need to get back to mine."

Nervous glances were exchanged around the table but no-one was willing to speak.

"But what about the people he cheated?" continued the dissenting juror. "Some of them have had their lives ruined?" The tenth juror sat back in her chair and looked around the room, hoping for some re-assurance or, perhaps, support.

"More fool them for believing a ridiculous story and putting their money into a skiing complex in Canada!" scoffed Yvonne. "The only guilty ones here are the investors. They are guilty of stupidity."

"It's Vicki, isn't it?" asked Hennie Raymond, looking across the table.

"Yes, Vicki Rollins," replied the mother of three young boys. She was comforted by his friendly smile.

"You're saying he's guilty and I respect that, Vicki. I don't agree with you, but what I would like to understand is how you have arrived at your conclusion?" he said.

"Enough of this," barked Yvonne. "I'm the foreman. Vicki, you'll..."

"Vicki should be given time to answer my question and I'd like you to act on my request," said Hennie. His stare convinced the local businesswoman to accede to him. With a somewhat arrogant waft of her bejewelled hand, she motioned her to continue.

"Well," said Vicki, "firstly, I didn't really like him and I don't think that I trust him, either." She stopped and looked around her. "He's got creepy eyes" she said.

"There speaks a woman scorned," said an unidentified voice.

David Williams' partner had added tomato sauce to his sandwich that she had made for him earlier that morning. He was becoming engrossed in the explanation being given by Vicki and he failed to notice that there were now four red splodges on the front of his light blue pullover.

"But I realise that is not enough of a basis for me to come to my decision." Vicki wiped her lips with a paper tissue. "I've thought about the evidence. It should be fairly easy to reach a decision." She hesitated and then reached for her bag. "I'm sorry. I'm a bit nervous. I've made some notes."

Yvonne was making eye contact with Nathan and was admiring his physical prowess. She raised her eyebrows and he nodded back.

"My first concern," said Vicki, and then stopped. Despite several audible groans from around the table she decided to continue reading from her piece of paper. "My worry is that it really isn't clear if this Maitland-Smith man had planning permission." She sipped some water from the paper cup that the juror to her right had slid in front of her. "I know that this sounds silly, but I'm not certain he owned the complex in the first place." She glanced at her notes before continuing. "To be honest, this stuff about a deferred purchase agreement went over my head."

"But Vicki, love. The investment document was signed off by a reputable firm of solicitors," interrupted Agnes Merton. She was a pensioner, a widow, a grandmother and was racked with arthritis in her feet and knees. That morning she had been late waking up, and had forgotten to take her tablets.

"Enough of this! I'm the foreman – unless anybody wants to challenge that?" bellowed Yvonne, who was now conscious she might be losing control of the conversation.

"You're the boss," said Nathan.

"We'll have another vote," ordered Yvonne, "and can I suggest," she said as she turned to Vicki, "that you put your notes away and follow the rest of us." She paused for a second or two, relishing her moment of authority. "Let's vote again. Please raise your hand if you think he's innocent."

Ten hands went up into the air. Yvonne raised her arm to make eleven.

A voice from the other end of the table asked, "Who thinks he's guilty?"

Vicki raised her arm.

"Eleven to one. This is ridiculous!" said Yvonne.

"Is there any chance you'll change your mind?" asked Dillon Masters.

Vicki turned to her right and looked down the table and into the face of her handsome fellow juror.

"We're here to reach a correct verdict," and then

she sneezed. "Sorry about that," she said as she rubbed her nose with the same paper tissue. The red-faced man to her left also needed to use his handkerchief which, Agnes decided, reminded her of a parachute on one of the 'Action Man' toys that her grandson loved playing with.

"All I'm saying," continued Vicki, "is that I think we owe it to the investors in Mr Maitland-Smith's scheme to discuss the evidence more thoroughly."

"I think Mr Maitland-Smith will be delighted if we find him innocent," said Dillon, eyeing Vicki's saddened face. He turned back to face the rest of the members, looking to share his opinion with his fellow jurors. "There are eleven of us who have reached that conclusion," he added.

"But what about all the people who lost their money?" stammered Vicki. She looked directly at him, "You know what I am saying." She paused. "I'm really not happy that we seem to be rushing to a decision."

"So one woman knows better than eleven other individuals. Is that what you are saying?" declared Dillon.

"Is the fact that I'm a woman troubling you?" asked Vicki.

"Why not ask the judge if he'll accept a majority verdict?" asked Lucas Mann.

"I would like to hear more from Vicki," said Agnes. She received a withering look from the foreman.

"No," said Yvonne. "We'll take a vote on whether we'll ask the judge if he'll accept an eleven to one vote." She stood up and looked down the table. "All in favour?"

Eight hands were raised into the air.

"Good enough for me," said Yvonne. "With me, that's nine. That's a majority."

Lucas hesitated. He was grappling with Yvonne's logic. Did it not need a unanimous vote before she should ask the judge, via the jury officer, if he would accept a majority vote? But events overtook him.

She went to the wall and pressed the buzzer. Everyone was now watching the end of the room and awaiting the arrival of the jury officer. After what seemed like an age, the door opened, there was a fairly long conversation and then a raised voice.

Back at the table, several of the jurors were exchanging opinions. Julian Crowe watched, with some amusement, as David Williams attempted to clean up the tomato sauce on his pullover only to leave a vivid stain across his chest.

The door closed and Yvonne returned to her chair.

"It's not that easy," she said. "If we want to ask the judge a question, what will happen is that the case he is presiding over will be stopped. We will be called to the waiting room. The judge will then summon Maitland-Smith, clerks and barristers and then us. He will then address the question we wish to ask, which will be explained by the clerk. The judge may make a decision immediately although it is possible that he may wish to talk separately to the lawyers." She paused and looked at Nathan who was silently applauding her.

"Basically, it sounds like a complete waste of time especially when we've only got ONE silly person holding everything up."

As Yvonne stressed the word 'one' she threw eyes like daggers towards Vicki who flinched and looked down to the floor beneath her feet.

"How long will that all take?" asked Hennie. He needed to make an urgent phone call. He was wondering whether, if they did return to court, he might be able to get hold of his mobile phone.

"It won't," answered Yvonne. "I told the clerk that we would reach a unanimous decision. I'm the foreman so that is what will happen. We're back to eleven versus one."

There was a lot of impatient shifting of chairs, legs and arms as most of the jurors stared at Vicki.

"I think he's guilty," she said.

"Is that all the clerk said?" asked Hennie.

"He said he thought that the judge would be annoyed that we had failed to follow his instructions. He's suggested we debate our decision more fully."

Yvonne looked at Nathan and narrowed her eyes.

Agnes smiled at Vicki and mouthed some words of encouragement.

Dillon had had enough. He turned his frustration onto the sole 'guilty' juror.

"Must be a real bundle of fun being married to you," he quipped.

Several of the jurors, including Hennie and Agnes, were unsettled by this attempt at levity.

"I'm not married," said Vicki.

"But you've got three children. As somebody said, it's all you talk about," continued Dillon.

"I was married but then I had reason to examine my husband and my life. He was a shit." She sipped some water. "You remind me of him in some ways," she said.

"We'll have a five minute break," ordered the foreman.

Hennie thought about Isobel. He wondered, yet again, whether her decision would be the one he wanted to hear. He remained exasperated that the jury officer had taken his phone from him.

Agnes spilled some water down her front as she took another tablet out of the prescription package and popped it into her mouth. She knew that the pain would start to ease in about half an hour's time, perhaps sooner. She saw that Vicki was looking at her. Agnes put down the cup and smiled back.

The tired-looking woman was puzzled. She resented the lack of direction she had been given. She had paid careful attention to the summing up by the judge and ended up more confused than ever. She had not taken to Yvonne and disliked her strident statements and lack of diplomacy. She felt that Vicki should be taken more seriously. Her baby kicked her and she felt a warming maternal glow inside.

Julian was thinking about politics. He was pondering how his hero, Nigel Farage, would have dealt with this impasse.

It was 11.17am on Friday morning.

The Jury

Yvonne Arrowsmith (f)

Red-faced older man (m)	Nathan Hercroil (m)
Vicki Rollins (f)	Hennie Raymond (m)
Julian Crowe (m)	Agnes Merton (f)
Tired-looking woman (f)	David Williams (m)
Lucas Mann (m)	Mrs Wainwright (f)

Dillon Masters (m)

Only three of the twelve jurors left the table and they soon returned having stretched their legs, which was some achievement given the cramped conditions. Several chatted amongst themselves, while the rest stayed silent, lost in their thoughts. Yvonne did not call the jurors to order but somehow the proceedings re-started.

"Can I propose," said Lucas "that we go through the evidence and try to identify the sections that are causing Vicki to arrive at her decision."

"What good will that do?" asked Nathan.

"I'm now a university researcher. I'm used to creating order from a range of documents. It's just a suggestion."

"It's a good one," agreed Hennie. He was silently cursing the absence of his phone. "What would she be thinking?" he pondered, as he recalled her scent.

"I think you'll find that I'm the foreman of this jury," protested Yvonne.

"Which is why you'll let our friend continue," Hennie retorted. He realised that Nathan was staring at him but remained steadfast.

"Thank you. My name is Lucas Mann. I was born in St Vincent and the Grenadines but I've lived here for over twenty years."

Agnes marvelled at his near perfect English accent. She decided that Lucas had been to a proper school. That mattered a great deal to Agnes.

"After leaving college I worked in a solicitor's office in Kingstown." He took out an immaculately ironed handkerchief and wiped his nose. "I was part of the corporate team that dealt with what you call 'off-shore' bank accounts."

"This is fascinating," commented Dillon, unable to

conceal his sarcasm.

Vicki looked at him. He reminded her of her ex-husband for another reason: he had Brad Pitt looks.

"No, please don't give up on me," said Lucas. "I'm trying to say that the profession that Mr Maitland-Smith works in is something I understand...can I continue... is that alright with everybody?"

"It's cool," said the tired-looking woman.

"Thank you...er... Miss."

As her baby was kicking her, she did not respond. No-one offered any other contribution, so Lucas continued.

"The facts of the case, as I understand them, are that the defendant calls himself a stockbroker and he has offices in the West End but I never really understood exactly what he does."

"Now, here's a fact that'll interest you all."

Lucas stopped as he was interrupted. Most of the jurors stared at Julian. The red-faced man was again coughing behind his cotton sheet.

"I thought that the prosecution barrister was ineffective," said Julian. "He put no real pressure on the defendant. But you might want to know this."

"Know what?" asked David Williams.

"I overheard them have a quick word when the judge's attention was diverted. I'm bloody sure they both went to Harrow School."

Yvonne banged her fist down on the table.

"This is getting out of hand. What on earth does...?"

"You're suggesting that the old-boy network means the prosecution didn't want try their best?" said Agnes.

"And worse. They could both be Masons!"

Julian sat back and savoured his moment of importance. As a member and financial backer of the anti-European political party, UKIP, he enjoyed having a dig at 'the Establishment'.

Hennie said nothing. He already knew the answer to the Masonic connection but actually didn't care. He was unable to tear himself away from wondering what decision Isobel might be making.

"Enough," shouted Yvonne. "Let's get back to the reality. I have decided to call for another vote: 'guilty' or 'not guilty'." She turned to her left and smiled. "Nathan, you go first, please," she said.

Nathan said "not guilty" as did the next three jurors. They all looked at Mrs Wainwright. She hesitated and paused for a few moments before announcing her decision. "Not guilty," she said.

The voting continued. Vicki stayed true to her 'guilty' vote and the count came in at eleven for 'not guilty' and one saying "guilty".

It was so nearly two, as one other juror was having doubts.

"I'll continue, shall I," said Lucas, as there was no direction from Yvonne other than her manifest exasperation. "Mr Maitland-Smith is a stockbroker and he was involved with what they call a 'cash shell'."

"I never understood that," commented Agnes.

"I think our interests are best served if we allow Lucas to finish off his summary," suggested Dillon. He was surprised that Vicki nodded in agreement.

"Mr Maitland-Smith did what we call 'reverse' a Canadian ski resort business into the shares." He hesitated. "I can explain that if you want." He looked around and decided to continue with his explanation of events. "The share price jumped from 2p to 17p in two weeks. We were told that he used a group of Mediterranean boiler rooms to sell the shares that he owned. The price of the shares escalated up to 32p in a period of seven weeks."

"What's a boiler room?" asked Yvonne.

"It's an offshore share selling scam," said Lucas. "The term 'offshore' means that the people operating the firms are based abroad – in this case in the Mediterranean area. This used to be Spain but these days they can be anywhere. The key point is that they are outside the jurisdiction of the financial regulators who control things in this country."

"Put it another way," jumped in Julian. "They use persuasive telephone techniques to sell worthless shares to people in this country who then expect us tax payers to recompense them for their loss. This is exactly what's wrong with…. "

Vicki raised her arm and Julian stopped in his tracks.

"Can I come in here, please?" she asked. "The prosecution made a big thing about the selling methods used by these boiler rooms. I was particularly interested by the statistic that over eighty per cent of the investors who had bought the shares were aged over sixty-five." She paused and then concluded, "I sensed there was a suggestion that these investors were bullied into it."

"But how does that make Maitland-Smith guilty?" asked Dillon. "He didn't make the phone calls."

"He was behind the calls," retorted Vicki. "Anyway," she continued – and then she stopped. After hesitating she took a deep breath and she confidently proclaimed that, "they also said that the share document was full of…" She lost her temporary gusto, grabbed her note pad, flicked a page and finished strongly by ending with, "full of ambiguities."

"But," said Agnes, "the shares were traded on a stock market. There was an application process." She hesitated as the pain in her right foot shot up her leg. "The lady barrister explained this rather well to us. Mr Maitland-Smith had completed all the required paperwork and a professional firm had signed everything off."

Vicki had also paid close attention to this part of the trial, which had taken place on the preceding Wednesday. The prosecution barrister spent some considerable time trying to prove that Mr Maitland-Smith had made false statements in the share trading application process. The defence team had reacted with theatrical and incredulous bemusement and Amanda Buckingham QC went through the checks, and what was referred to as the 'due diligence' process, to show that her client was innocent of all charges.

"If I may I'll carry on, ladies and gentlemen," said Lucas. "Over the next seven months the share price fluctuated and then an investment website, which follows risky shares, announced that the climate change effect in Northern America had resulted in adverse skiing conditions and the closure of some of the main pistes. As a result of this new information, the price of the individual properties collapsed. The shares had fallen to 8p when the stock market suspended trading. At that point the financial regulator stepped in and announced it was investigating the company and Geoffrey Maitland-Smith." He paused and scanned his notes. "It was found that he had been selling shares, through the boiler rooms, all the time they were rising and his profit had been calculated to be around twenty-four million pounds."

"Did he carry on selling shares when he already knew about the changing conditions in Canada and the falling value of the chalets?" asked David Williams, who was now a little less concerned about his stained jumper.

The jurors generally sat still as they pondered this question and they absorbed Lucas's summary. It had been a messy trial. The defence barrister seemed to have licence to interrupt proceedings whenever she chose. She also tended to focus on several of the male members of the jury whenever she was speaking.

"Great summary, Lucas," said Julian. "I'm sorry about the investors' losses, but this was obviously a questionable investment. The document gave out all the warnings, so I'm asking of what crime was Maitland-Smith guilty?"

"What do you mean, 'sorry about the investors'?" asked Mrs Wainwright.

"They bought risky shares. More fool them!" replied Julian.

"We'll have a break. I need to use the facilities," said the foreman. She was followed into the washrooms by the red-faced older man who stumbled over a chair.

It was 12.19pm on Friday lunchtime.

"Sorry about what I said, it wasn't a nice thing to have said to you."

Vicki turned her gaze away from the view out of the window, such as it was, and looked at Dillon.

"I was wrong to say you're a shit," she said.

He laughed.

"Perhaps you're right," he said. "How old are your children?" he asked.

"Noah is nine, Jack is seven and Charlie is my baby. He's two."

"That's a gap," he commented.

"Two fathers," said Vicki.

Dillon nodded as he raised his eyebrows.

There was a small commotion in the room as Yvonne, who had now returned, moved her chair closer to Nathan and tapped the top of the table.

"Time's pressing. I want to have another vote," she announced.

The jurors settled down and she began the count. "'Not guilty', 'not guilty', 'not guilty', 'not guilty', 'not guilty', 'not guilty', 'not guilty', 'not guilty', 'not guilty', 'guilty' and I'm 'not guilty' so we're still at eleven to one" said the foreman, having ignored juror eleven.

"Guilty'.

All heads turned towards the red-faced older man.

"Why?" yelled Dillon.

"I don't need to give a reason," he stuttered.

He was unable to continue speaking because, once again as his fellow jurors averted their gaze he appeared to be having trouble with his breathing. Mrs Wainwright however was watching him carefully as she felt that all was not as it seemed as she could see a stain on his handkerchief.

"Ten to two," said Hennie.

"I want to change my vote," said Agnes, "but I'm hesitating."

"You, as well?" asked Dillon with a frustrated gasp.

"As Vicki said earlier, you really are odious!" She repositioned herself on her chair. The prescription was now working and the pain in her lower joints was receding.

"Listening to Lucas brought my concerns back to the surface. The point was made earlier that there is some doubt about whether this Maitland-Smith man had planning permission and, as Vicki said, we're not sure that he had ownership of the properties. He had acquired title with what we were told was a deferred purchase agreement. The defence never proved he had paid for the properties."

"May I please ask a question?" said David Williams. "What's he guilty of?"

"The charge is..." began Hennie.

"I'm not interested in the charge," he said. "Vicki. You have voted 'guilty' every time. What is Maitland-Smith guilty of?"

"Fraud," said Vicki. Jack, her middle son, could not say his 'r's. He would have pronounced it 'fward'.

What they did not know was that another juror had, in the last few moments, decided to vote differently. There was a knock at the door and four jurors were served their rather uninspiring lunches. Three had ordered lasagne, one a panini ... .no-one ended up happy with their choice.

As the smell of recently microwaved food wafted and dominated the air, Mrs Wainwright couldn't stop her thoughts going back to her decision to invest in a Vietnamese agricultural scheme. It had started with a phone call from a rather pleasant young man called Benjamin. He immediately disclosed that he was a share salesman but, initially, seemed more interested in her personal circumstances; her second career as a teacher; her grandchildren; and, her decision to vote for Brexit. He disagreed with that but praised her for the way in which she argued her point of view. He always called her 'Mrs Wainwright'. He sent her some forms that she showed to one of her friend at her Pilates class. She completed the paperwork and opened an account to become a client of Anglo-Capital Limited. She decided to discuss the matter with her husband but, as usual, he was pre-occupied with his work.

She told Benjamin that she had little spare money and that he should not waste his time with her. He replied that he had become more interested in their daily telephone chats. She could not recall how he discovered that she had a pension as a former teacher. He sent her details of a scheme whereby she could cash in part, or all, of the fund. She read up carefully on the detail and contacted her pension provider. Within five weeks she received the sum of twenty-nine thousand pounds. Benjamin told her that she should lock the money away in the bank. However she was frustrated by the low rate of interest they offered on her deposit.

There was no doubt in her mind that Benjamin had awakened her repressed sexual frustrations. There were days when she sat by the phone waiting for his call. He had the knack of making her feel rather seductive. He was never crude; just suggestive.

Her husband was forever involved in things that mattered more than any other priority in their lives. Time and again she visited the grandchildren on her own. She had a decent standard of living and, even without her pension, was financially comfortable. She was a governor of her old school and enjoyed the meetings of the trustees.

Benjamin began talking to her about an opportunity to double or even treble her money. She had to remind him about it when, for several days, he did not mention it. He sent her a brochure, stunningly illustrated, about an investment opportunity in Vietnam. She read every word of the documentation and researched the country background. After two weeks of daily discussions about risk and reward she emailed Benjamin a completed application form and went into her bank and transferred twenty-five thousand pounds to Anglo-Capital Limited.

The telephone calls stopped immediately. Benjamin's number was discontinued and the email address closed down. She went into London and, in the back streets of Highgate, she could only find an accommodation address operated by an aggressive Pakistani taxi driver.

She told no-one about the situation and shed her tears in private. Her husband paid an allowance into her account each month and she had her state pension. She was left with a bank deposit account containing four thousand pounds.

The problem she faced was that she felt humiliated. Many hours were taken up as she revisited every single phone call with Benjamin. She re-read all the documentation. She knew that he had played on her sexual frustration. She remembered the occasion when he asked her what she was wearing. After that she always made sure that she dressed appropriately for when he phoned her. She concluded that she was a stupid, ageing woman. She decided to tell her husband.

She thought that he over-reacted to her loss. He did not take long to work out what approach Benjamin had taken. Mrs Wainwright tried to understand his angst and went to great lengths to explain the research she had undertaken before committing her funds. Nothing she said appeased Detective Inspector Wainwright. One evening, after several drinks too many, the atmosphere became barbed. She could not understand his logic. He was repeatedly telling her that he had one year to go to his retirement and she had humiliated him. Then he hit her.

The next morning she found a handwritten letter of apology awaiting her on the kitchen table. They had not referred to the matter again and their lives returned to some level of normality. She knew that her friend at the Pilates class had not believed her explanation for the bruising on the side of her face. She was forever feeling her chipped tooth with her tongue.

She had carried her sense of self-reproach with her into court every day. Almost from the start of the evidence being heard she concluded that the investors in the Canadian skiing complex were all as stupid as she had been, but now she could not take her eyes off Vicki. She respected her courage in standing up to the rest of the jurors and admired her spirit. Then the reality of her experience became clearer. She had taken all the responsibility for her financial loss on her own shoulders.

"It was Benjamin who defrauded me," she thought to herself. "It's my husband, who pays me no attention, who caused me to grasp at a silly period of flirtation."

She stood up and walked over to the window. She found that she was standing by Julian. He turned to her and spoke quietly.

"I hope you don't mind me saying but I can't help but notice, since the case started, what a lovely dress sense you have." He smiled. "You always have such presence," he oozed.

Mrs Wainwright returned to her seat. She was sixty-two years old. She looked over at Vicki and wondered about what had just been said. He had used the word 'presence'. He would never know what that meant to her. She was now beginning to feel sixty-two years' young. She had been the victim of a fraudster. She breathed in deeply as she began the process of planning her next five years.

She was annoyed with herself. She should have joined Vicki for the second count and found Mr Geoffrey Maitland-Smith 'guilty'. She had hesitated; now she was sure.

"For me," said Nathan, "what matters is whether this dude Maitland-Smith intended to defraud the suckers." He looked to his right as he realised that Yvonne had placed her hand on his sleeve. "The blonde one, defence person, made some good points. It wasn't his fault that the fucking snow melted."

"That's not right," said Vicki. "There's a section in the document about climatic issues."

"Darlin'," interrupted Nathan, patronisingly, "it's bloody clear to us all that you's got a lemon on any prick with money."

"What on earth does that mean?" said Agnes.

"What Nathan is suggesting," said Julian, "is that

he thinks Vicki resents people who have more money than her."

"That's not fair!" cried Vicki incredulously. "I accept my lot. My children never go without."

"You called 'im a 'shit'," continued Nathan, looking at Dillon. He was now resting his hand on top of Yvonne's arm. "We've all seen his wheels and the looker who picks 'im up outside the court. What's it cost, brother?"

Dillon smiled.

"It's a Lamborghini Huracan. I paid around eighty thousand pounds for it."

"Did that include the bird?" laughed Nathan.

"That is Margaritta," said Dillon. "She's my driver. She gets me around."

"Good for da image, dude," suggested Nathan.

"I suppose so," he said and then added, "together with the fact that I've lost my driving licence."

"How have you made your obvious wealth?" asked Agnes.

"I haven't. My father has built up a company that supplies the defence industry. Bit hush-hush. He gave my two sisters and me a great start in life with private schooling, holiday homes and the rest. Eleanor works in publishing and Jackie is in Australia working for Sky News." He paused, smiled and looked at Vicki. "I'm already a shit, so not too much point in trying to impress you," he said. "I live off my father. I've some investment properties." He maintained his gaze in her direction, "My guess is that I'm everything you resent in life."

"You're bloody honest," said the tired-looking woman.

"We have an Executive Box at the Emirates,"

added Dillon.

Vicki could not afford the Arsenal shirts for her sons.

It was 1.22pm on Friday.

Yvonne squeezed Nathan's hand and removed it so that she could tap the surface of the table. She announced that she wanted a further vote to decide whether Geoffrey Maitland-Smith was guilty or not. She looked at Nathan and the count began. 'Not guilty', 'Not guilty' and then there was a pause. All eyes focused on Agnes. She looked around the table and hesitated. "Guilty," she said as she smiled at Vicki.

Yvonne looked towards the ceiling and inwardly groaned. She asked David Williams for his decision. He was trying to hide his tomato sauce stain by leaning his elbow on the table and resting his chin between finger and thumb. "Not guilty," he said.

Mrs Wainwright was feeling elated. This was a special moment for her because it was the first occasion when she had felt liberated from her ordeal of the past few weeks.

"Guilty," she said.

There was a stunned silence as the other jurors registered another change of mind. Yvonne moved on and asked Dillon for his vote. He looked at Vicki.

"Sorry," he said. "I almost want to vote with you. I like your stance. But I can't." He smiled at her.

"Definitely Brad Pitt," she thought to herself as she nodded her appreciation of his words.

"Not guilty," he said.

He was followed by Lucas who maintained his opinion. "Not guilty," he said.

The tired-looking woman said 'not guilty', as did Julian.

Vicki repeated her vote of 'guilty' and was followed by the red-faced older man with the same opinion. He then had another coughing fit which he barely was able to contain in his blotchy handkerchief.

Yvonne said she remained a 'not guilty' vote, which made it eight for 'not guilty' and four for 'guilty'.

Julian raised his hand and reacted to Yvonne's nod of her head.

"I wonder, Chairman, if I might comment on what is taking place. I'll try not to ruffle any feathers but, as I understand what is happening, is it possible that we're losing sight of the task we face. We are being asked to decide whether Geoffrey Maitland-Smith is guilty of fraud. I share the view expressed that the prosecuting counsel was weak and the defence was, shall we say, entertaining. The judge was clearly trying to be even-handed in his summing up and gave us no real clear direction."

"Where is this going?" asked David Williams.

"I want to pose a question. I'm thinking that we're losing sight of the evidence and concentrating more on the issue of personal circumstances."

"I'm even more lost," exclaimed Yvonne.

"In my opinion," continued Julian Crowe, "the evidence presented does not justify a decision of 'guilty' and remember the count was eleven to one when Yvonne took the first vote." He paused and smiled. "Then Vicki made a stand. Now I have to be careful in what I say." He looked at the mother of three boys. "You really are a gentle-looking woman and your understated mannerisms are compelling.

Perhaps you don't realise but, somehow, and I don't for one moment think you meant this, you've captured a protest vote. Several of you are voting 'guilty' because you are judging Geoffrey Maitland-Smith on his wealth and personal circumstances. He's made twenty-four million pounds from this venture and you don't like that."

The silence which engulfed the room was broken by Agnes.

"Quite a speech," she said.

"Crap," said David Williams. "I'm off work and me and my partner have debts." He paused. "Loads of debts, to be honest. I voted 'not guilty' on the evidence."

"I thought you said that you're a school teacher?" said Vicki.

"Primary school teacher," he answered.

"So why are you not working?" asked Dillon.

"There was a misunderstanding with a pupil," he muttered.

Mrs Wainwright leaped to her feet and rushed to the other end of the table.

She reached the red-faced older man who was breathing heavily and had slumped down in his chair. She loosened his collar and recoiled as she faced a wave of a chemical odour.

"Is it a heart attack?" asked Yvonne as she moved towards the buzzer on the wall.

Dillon had rushed out of the toilet, slopping drops of water from a hastily-filled beaker.

"Nothing of the sort," she said. "He's drunk." She waved a small hip-flask that had slipped out of his pocket as he collapsed.

"But what's that smell?" asked Yvonne, as she

fought her way through the peering crowd of jurors.

"He's using a chemical mouthwash to disguise his drinking," said Dillon. "Let's get some coffee down him." He paused. "If we lose him we'll be coming back on Monday."

The red-faced man was propped back in his chair, protesting that he had experienced a funny turn through not eating. As he did so, he patted his right trouser pocket to find his hip-flask was not there. He gazed at the table and there it was in front of him. Nothing further was said as Mrs Wainwright picked it up, smiled and popped it into her handbag.

The red-faced man was now riddled with embarrassment as he tried to sink back into his chair.

No-one else said anything; nothing at all; everyone was being rather British about it but, as the silence began to get awkward, Yvonne sensed it was her opportunity to claw back control.

She announced that the vote was now eight for 'not guilty' and four for 'guilty'.

"Not so," said Lucas, "I'm changing my vote."

"Seven, five," said Yvonne. "Let's have a break."

Vicki went to the toilet, returned to the jury room and moved cautiously towards the owner of the Lamborghini, who seemed lost in his thoughts. He smiled at her.

"I know I'm a spoilt shit," he said.

"And I'm a left wing zealot who hates the rich," laughed Vicki as she sat down.

"Did that guy have a point?" he asked as he turned to face her. "Do you resent what I am?"

"Of course," she said. "I want the best for my boys. I'd love to take them to see Arsenal play but

I've not much money. Both the fathers are contributing so I'm better off than some. My mortgage is being paid. But my allowance and benefits are all but spent the moment they come into my account." She paused. "My father had to help me out last month. It's a rotten way to live your life." She hesitated and then continued. "In truth, I think Julian made a good point." She smiled. "I'm studying for a book-keeping qualification at college. I've one examination to pass and then I should be able to find work."

Dillon stared at her and nodded in admiration.

"You're rather attractive," said Dillon. "Perhaps the right man is out there."

"I've thought that twice," she said.

It was 2.43pm on Friday afternoon.

"So, where do we go from here?" asked Hennie. He desperately needed to reach his phone. The bank officials were threatening to close down his business and he had found a possible investor. They had become quite close as Isobel learned more about him and his business activities. She said she was going to speak to her solicitor and he should phone her before the weekend. She had not answered her phone first thing that morning and he had reached a point in time where he did not care whether Geoffrey Maitland-Smith was innocent or guilty. He had spent twenty-odd years of his life building his transportation business but in the last two years, with greater foreign competition, the increasing cost of the minimum wage and the spiralling rise in insurance premiums, he had faced increasing cash flow pressures.

Recently things had gone from bad to worse when

he had been unable to release five lorries caught up in the migrant camp riots at Calais and their loads of perishable goods had been condemned. The insurance company was pointing to a 'force-majeure' clause in the agreement and disputing payment of his claim.

He decided that Vicki was not going to change her mind and he didn't care. He needed Isobel's investment or he'd be thrown on the scrap heap, just like his stock had been.

Yvonne was becoming more and more inseparable from Nathan as they whispered and giggled away like besotted teenagers. She did, however, now drag herself away from him, tap the table top and suggest yet another vote.

Nathan voted 'not guilty', only to hear that Hennie had changed his decision and said, quietly, "guilty." Agnes looked amazed and added a further 'guilty' vote. David Williams repeated his 'not guilty' decision. Mrs Wainwright said, "Guilty," and Dillon looked at Vicki and mouthed, "Sorry". His vote was 'not guilty'. Lucas, for the first time, said, "Guilty," and the tired-looking woman voted 'not guilty'. Julian seemed to hesitate and looked at Hennie, "Not guilty," he said. Vicki smiled and raised her hand.

Yvonne said that she'd take that as a 'guilty' vote.

The red-faced older man sheepishly muttered one word while avoiding any eye contact: "Guilty," he stammered.

Yvonne was now taking notes as she was becoming more confused.

"That's six of us saying 'not guilty' and six voting 'guilty' she announced. "The judge said we must reach a decision by 4.30pm or we come back on Monday."

She paused. "I suggest a five minute break for all of us to think through where we go from here."

It was 2.56pm on Friday afternoon.

The tired-looking woman hoped that she would not be returning on Monday. She would go to the clinic and try to be released. She had found some blood when she had used the toilet a little earlier and she was becoming distinctly uninterested in the matter of whether Geoffrey Maitland-Smith was guilty or not. She recalled the classic movie she had watched the other Sunday while her boyfriend slept off the effects of his traditional Saturday night – 'Gone with the Wind' – and that famous line:

"Frankly, my dear, I don't give a damn."

She laughed inwardly as she remembered that Clark Gable was speaking his last words to Vivien Leigh after she had asked him, "What shall I do?"

She said to herself.

"Frankly, Mr Maitland-Smith, I don't give a damn."

Yvonne and Nathan were engaged in yet another furtive and increasingly intense conversation. Yvonne shared with him that she was building up a property letting business but was plagued by irresponsible tenants. Some of their behaviour was unbelievable and the state of several of the vacated homes defied belief. She bemoaned the number of solicitors' letters that had been issued and unanswered. She ridiculed the system which acted slowly enough to allow former tenants to escape the legal net.

Nathan suggested that there was another way to control matters. He'd had enough of driving trains and forever being put under pressure to manage arrival times within the guidelines. He suggested to Yvonne that she might employ him as her 'fixer'. She said that she had three addresses for him to visit that evening. They indulged in another whispered conversation and agreed they'd go for a drink as soon as they were out of the court, to talk through their fledgling partnership.

Yvonne realised that other conversations that had been going on around the table were coming to an end. She drummed the surface with her fingers and said, "Look, it is getting late and we've all got places to go." She smiled towards Vicki as she added, "With children to spend time with…if everyone is ready let's vote again".

Vicki smiled back and nodded her agreement and Yvonne turned to Nathan.

"Guilty," he said.

Hennie looked surprised but maintained his position of 'guilty'. Agnes voted 'guilty' and David Williams said, "Not guilty". Mrs Wainwright said, "Guilty," and Dillon asked Yvonne to let him think for a moment. Lucas said, "Guilty," and the tired-looking woman changed her vote: "guilty," she muttered. Several eyebrows were raised at this last vote. Julian said, "Not guilty," followed by Vicki who said, "Guilty." The red-faced older man had now seemed a little more awake as he said he wanted to maintain his vote as 'guilty'.

Yvonne asked Dillon for his decision which he confirmed as 'not guilty'.

She said that her vote was now 'guilty'. This made the overall count as nine voting 'guilty' and three saying 'not guilty'.

Hennie lifted his fist and brought it down firmly

on the surface of the table. He needed to speak to the potential investor in his business.

Yvonne looked surprised.

"So we're at nine for 'guilty' and three who are saying 'not guilty'," she said.

Hennie was becoming more and more impatient. He had worked unbelievably hard to build his business and he felt sure that his pitch to Isobel had been fruitful but he needed to hear her decision. He looked around the room. There were three jurors preventing a unanimous vote. He wondered who was the weakest: David Williams, Dillon or Julian.

"I can't see the point in coming back on Monday," said David Williams. "I don't really feel strongly one way or the other. I'll change my vote to 'guilty'."

Hennie sighed in relief. Two votes to change.

"I'll join you," said Julian. "I have a very important political conference over the weekend and I don't want this over my head."

Yvonne clenched Nathan's hand in relief. They were already furthering their plans for a series of visits he might make to selected tenants.

"Just you, Dillon" she said. "If you'll change your vote I'll call the officer and tell him."

Dillon looked at the foreman and then around the room. He came to rest when his gaze reached Vicki.

"Not guilty," he said.

"And you aren't going to change your mind, are you Dillon?" asked Vicki.

"Never," he replied.

It was 3.14pm on Friday afternoon.

The vote now stood at eleven for 'guilty' and one for 'not guilty'.

In an attempt to break the paralysing silence that seemed to have engulfed the room, one juror decided to try to take the lead.

"Would I be right in thinking that nobody wants to have to return on Monday?" asked Dillon.

The tired-looking woman already knew that she didn't want to come back to the court room.

"If it will help, I'll change my vote to 'not guilty'," she said.

Dillon smiled and wrote on the piece of paper in front of him. He looked to the far end of the table.

"Yvonne and Nathan. You changed your votes rather abruptly. Why not change back?"

"If it helps, that's what we'll do," said Yvonne. "I've lost my way on all of this. Nathan and I have business to attend to." She put her hand on his. "Not guilty," she said, "and that goes for Nathan."

Dillon added two more ticks to the names on his piece of paper.

"You're going to an important UKIP meeting, aren't you?" he asked Julian.

"Not guilty," replied the wannabe political activist.

"Let's hope you'll be discussing the fairness of our judicial system," said Agnes.

"Ouch," said Julian. "I get your drift," he said smiling at his fellow juror sitting opposite him. "Let's be straight about this. We've had no real direction about this trial. The court room events were clouded by a poor prosecution and, I for one, did not get a clear direction from the judge's summary." He paused and sipped some water. "If Maitland-Smith is found guilty he'll get a suspended sentence. Our prisons are crowded out with record numbers of inmates because of the way we have let immigration run riot in this country. This stockbroker, who we are trying, will keep all the money anyway." He hesitated. "I want to do the right thing but I genuinely believe our verdict will not make much difference. So I am taking a pragmatic view." He looked around him. "I say 'not guilty' and that's final."

Dillon added a further tick to his analysis. He wondered if the foreman wanted to take the lead but she had been down-graded in the role.

"That's seven votes for 'guilty' and five of us saying 'not guilty'," advised Dillon.

"I'm changing my vote," said Agnes, looking across the table. "I hear what you say," she said to Julian. "Not guilty," she announced.

"I'm also changing."

Several jurors stared at Mrs Wainwright. She looked around the table.

"I'll be honest. I don't want to come back next week. I want to visit my grandchildren. If the most he'll get is a suspended sentence, I don't see what good it will do prolonging matters." To some extent her regained self-confidence was wavering.

Dillon added to his notes a further tick making the count five for 'guilty' and seven siding with him. He had written down four names – Hennie, David Williams, Lucas and Vicki – when his task was made easier. The red-faced older man spoke up.

"I've got my meeting on Monday. I say 'not guilty'."

Hennie was lost in his thoughts. He needed Isobel's money and he rather hoped that her intended investment might strengthen their relationship.

"Not guilty," he said.

Dillon added a further tick to his list and

wondered who was the weakest of the remaining three jurors voting 'guilty'. He was in no doubt that Vicki was the strongest. He was warming to her as the afternoon took its toll of them all. He was not to know that Vicki was missing Charlie and she would not be seeing him until Monday.

David Williams and Lucas were looking at each other across the table and imperceptibly nodding. Lucas suggested a further vote was taken and Yvonne extracted herself from Nathan's attention and completed the task. She asked each juror to confirm their vote. Nathan had said, "Not guilty," before she had finished talking and was followed by Hennie.

Agnes confirmed her 'not guilty' vote as did David Williams.

Mrs Wainwright was struggling. Recalling her husband's regular rants about how there was not enough space in our prisons for convicted attackers and worse and having heard the grunts of agreement for Julian's comments she said reluctantly she was voting 'not guilty'.

Dillon laughed and raised his hand. Lucas said, "Not guilty," and the tired-looking woman raised her arm.

"Not guilty?" asked Yvonne and the tired-looking woman nodded her head; she was being to feel decidedly unwell.

Yvonne moved on to Julian who said, "Not guilty."

All eyes focused on Vicki.

"Come back to me," she said.

The red-faced older man had now nodded off to sleep and had to be woken up which the foreman undertook with a not-too-gentle bang on the table.

"Er...not guilty," he spluttered as he reached for his handkerchief, only to recall that he'd been deprived of its not-so-secret contents.

"I'm voting 'not guilty'," she said. "That means there are eleven of us saying the same thing." She looked at Vicki. "Just your decision to make, please," she said.

In dealing with two failed marriages and bringing up three boys, Vicki had learned never to rush. Each decision, each moment, each relationship, all needed careful thought. She was proud that she had come out of her tunnel of despair with her family around her and the bills all paid. She was lonely, but she instinctively believed that around the corner better times lay ahead. She wanted to return to Jack, Noah and Charlie. That is where she belonged. She'd have to wait until Monday when she would have them all back. She had stood her ground and believed that her initial stance had led to a more thorough debate on whether Mr Maitland-Smith was guilty or not. Vicki silently patted herself on the back. She had done her duty. She looked around and found that Dillon was watching her. He smiled and she melted inside.

"Not guilty," she said.

Silence erupted around the room with shrugs of shoulders and perplexed looks. No-one knew what to do next as it slowly dawned on each and every juror that after nearly a week in the company of strangers they were shortly to be free of one and all.

Yvonne leaped up and pressed the buzzer on the wall. She advised the jury officer that they had reached a unanimous decision and turned to all those behind her. With exuberant pomposity, she declared, "I'd like to thank you all for the support you have given to me in what was not an easy matter, but I think I was able to keep us all on track and I got us there in the end". The words fell on deaf ears and Yvonne was a little more than a bit upset that there were no words of appreciation or thanks. She grabbed Nathan's arm.

The Jury Officer nodded and suggested that they prepare to return and advise the judge of their verdict. When they reached the court they found that the immaculately-dressed Geoffrey Maitland-Smith seemed to be enjoying a conversation with his defence barrister.

It was 4.11pm on Friday.

Hennie became increasingly frustrated by further delays in the court proceedings but was finally able to speak to his potential investor. He heard the news that he was dreading. Isobel would not be investing and she declined his offer of dinner that evening. He sloped away, shoulders drooped and head down. He did not know where he was going.

The red-faced older man reached the pub at 5.25pm later that afternoon. He lasted until around nine o'clock when an ambulance was called to take him to the local hospital after he'd fallen off his chair and hit his head on the floor. He never made it to his meeting on Monday.

The tired-looking woman lost her baby on the Sunday afternoon. She lay alone in the hospital bed as the father failed to show despite her text messages pleading for him to come to her aid. Her mother was out on the town with yet another new man.

Agnes and Mrs Wainwright continued their growing friendship. There was a mutual benefit in that the policeman's wife was rather informative on curative diets and was able to suggest a basis for improving Agnes's pain relief in her legs. For her part, Agnes was able to offer Mrs Wainwright a new friendship based not only on the enforced coming together, but the shared experience. Agnes' neighbour was a dentist and they agreed to meet for a coffee next week so she could pass on the details. Mrs Wainwright found herself fingering her face where the tooth was chipped but doing so with a smile, and not a grimace, for the first time in weeks and she stayed married but not happily.

Yvonne and Nathan lasted less than a week together. The pugilistic methods employed by her new associate proved too much for her basic business values. She replaced Nathan with membership of the Association of Residential Lettings Agents. She read their material and attended several training courses and after several months her business began to prosper. Nathan ended up being involved in another jury trial but this time as the defendant when a disagreement in a late night kebab shop got out of hand. There was a guilty verdict on this occasion.

Lucas and Julian went their individual ways, both successfully. David Williams won his appeal and returned to teaching. He secured a position at another school and he still has a sausage sandwich every morning.

As he walked out of the Crown Court buildings, Dillon spotted a Lamborghini parked on a double yellow line. Margaritta was wearing a red cap. He realised that Vicki was at his side.

"Smart car," she said.

"That was a difficult moment for you, wasn't it?" said Dillon.

"Do you think that I was weak?" she asked.

He faced her and put his arms on her shoulders.

"Because of you, Mr Maitland-Smith received a fair hearing. That's why we were there, wasn't it?"

Vicki looked at the playboy and smiled.

"I must say you really are a decent shit," she laughed.

"Tell me," he asked, "If I was a neighbour of yours without the wealth, the cars and the women, would I stand any chance of having a dinner date with you?"

Vicki smiled and put her hand on his arm.

"Let me understand the question," she said. "The way you've just manipulated us in there tells me I need to be careful."

They had now stopped and were sitting on a wall. Margaritta appeared to be having an argument with a traffic warden.

"You, Dillon Masters, are, in truth, an everyday bloke with an everyday job and you want me to have dinner with you."

"Expressed with your usual formidable simplicity," laughed Dillon.

"The answer's 'no," said Vicki.

Dillon felt crestfallen. The days in her company had convinced him that here was someone a bit special.

"But," continued Vicki, "it might be possible to elicit a different reply."

"Conditions?" asked Dillon.

"Not really," said Vicki. "If Dillon Masters, trainee decent man, and, I may say, rather attractive, was to

40

ask Vicki Rollins, divorced mother of three boys, if she was able, this weekend, to drive him into the countryside in his Lamborghini, there might be an affirmative response."

"I can't get three boys safely into the car," said Dillon.

"They'll be with their fathers. We have a monthly arrangement. They were collected this afternoon. I'll have two days to myself." She hesitated, "I'll miss them dreadfully but I have a responsibility to give them time with their dads."

"I can't have children," said Dillon.

Vicki raised her eyebrows in surprise.

"I've done the married act. All she wanted was children. In the end I agreed to be tested and it was me. She left me shortly afterwards."

"You're full of surprises. Where does Margaritta fit in?"

"She works for my father and drives me around." He stood up. "Have you driven a Lamborghini?" he asked.

"I've two of them in the garage," she sassily quipped.

"Let me get this right," said Dillon but he had to pause. Margaritta had driven round the block and was now blowing the horn of the car in a mixture of temper and frustration. Dillon ran down the steps and there was a brief conversation. The Lamborghini disappeared in a haze of smoke resulting from the wheel spin. He returned to his fellow juror who was sending a text message. He smiled at her.

"If Dillon Masters, wealthy playboy and luxury car owner, was to request the pleasure of Vicki Rollins for a weekend away, might there be an affirmative answer?"

"Possibly," said Vicki. She noted that a day had become a weekend.

"What now?" asked Dillon.

"No Margaritta," said Vicki.

"Not a problem," said Dillon, "this weekend, she'll be driving my father to Ascot."

They stood up and she looked at him.

"You do have a style about you, Dillon," she said. "I'm going to catch the bus home."

"Can I come?" he asked. "I haven't been on a bus in years."

Vicki looked at him.

"You've never had a weekend away with a girl like me, have you?" she said.

"I'll let you know the verdict on that on Sunday evening," he laughed.

They started to walk down the steps towards the bus-stop when Dillon stopped and turned to face her.

"Tomorrow week, Saturday," he said, "Arsenal are at home. They're playing Chelsea." He paused. "My father always allows me six tickets for the box."

Vicki paused and smiled.

THE END

NOTE: The story of '12 Angry Men'

The 1957 film is set in a New York courthouse. It tells of the events as twelve men (the jury) deliberate on whether an 18-year-old Hispanic youth is guilty of stabbing his father to death.

It has two unusual features. Firstly, all but three of the ninety-six minutes of screening take place in the jury room. Secondly, only two names are revealed. At the conclusion, on the steps of the building, Juror 8 (played by Henry Fonda) is revealed as 'Davis' and Juror 9 (Joseph Sweeney) is 'McCardle'. The defendant is referred to 'the boy'.

Juror 1 (played by Martin Balsam) is the foreman. He calls for a vote. Eleven vote 'guilty' with Henry Fonda, the one doubter, arguing that the destiny of 'the boy' deserves some deliberation. As it is a criminal trial the verdict must be unanimous. Tensions show almost immediately. Juror 7 (Jack Warden) has tickets for the evening's Yankee game and Juror 10 (played by Ed Begley) reveals a blatant prejudice against people from the slums.

Juror 3 (Lee J Cobb) is stubborn and possesses a violent temper. Juror 4 (E G Marshall) is a stockbroker and is concerned with the facts and Juror 12 (Robert Webber) is a wisecracking advertising executive.

The film is dominated by Henry Fonda. He maintains a dignified persistence in exposing doubts about the two witnesses. He repeats that if there is 'reasonable doubt' then they must find that 'the boy' is 'not guilty'. As the afternoon drags on he maintains his stance, politely questioning the facts and other jurors' motives. Finally, one by one, the eleven men change their initial opinion and the defendant is found 'not guilty.'

The genius of the film lies in the performance of Henry Fonda and his interaction with the varying personalities. He manages conflict and tension in his unique way. He performs brilliantly throughout. It was shot in three weeks. Fonda co-produced the movie although he later said that he would never produce a film again.

'12 Angry Men' was adapted from his own teleplay by Reginald Rose who also co-produced it. The director was Sidney Lumet and it was the first of his fifty feature films. It was a box office disappointment but went on to gain numerous awards. Lumet had greater success in 1982 with 'The Verdict', a courtroom drama starring Paul Newman.

Henry Fonda (16 May 1905-12 August 1982) is particularly remembered for 'The Grapes of Wrath' and his last film 'On Golden Pond'. In 1999 he was named the sixth-Greatest Male Star of All Time by the American Film Institute. In May 2005 the United States Post Office issued a 37-cent postage stamp depicting an artist's drawing of the film legend.

-0-

Look out for more in the 'Novella Nostalgia' series

If you would like to be notified when the next book is released, be sure to sign up for my free newsletter at:

tonydruryemailsign-up.gr8.com

ALSO BY TONY DRURY

Sarah Rudd City Thriller series

Sarah Rudd stories

Sarah Rudd Short Stories

Stories written for HEART UK – The Cholesterol Charity. (All publisher's profits are paid to the charity)

Hannah's Choice

Joanna's Choice: getBook.at/JoannasChoice

Mark's Choice: getBook.at/MarksChoice

The Dinner Party

The Novella Nostalgia Series

Lunch with Harry

THE NOVELLA NOSTALGIA SERIES

This publishing initiative brings together the uniqueness of the novella and various memorable movies from the history of cinema.

The word 'novella' comes from the Italian for 'novel.' It has been interpreted in various ways including 'a long short story' or a 'short novel'. It can be traced back to the early renaissance in Italy and France. Giovanni Boccaccio wrote 'The Decameron' in 1353. This comprises 100 tales of ten people fleeing the black death. It was not until the 18th and 19th centuries that the novella emerged as a literary genre.

In 1941, the Austrian novelist Stefan Zweig wrote 'The Chess Novella' which was later renamed 'The Royal Game'. This was the inspiration for the 1960 film 'Brainwashed'.

Most modern novellas are published by Penguin Modern Classics. The various novella prizes seem to stipulate a word count of between 7,500 and 40,000. A key feature of the novella is its limited punctuation. There are no chapter headings and no breaks apart from spaces where the author needs to show a scene change.

-0-

'Lunch with Harry' pays tribute to one of the great films produced by Hollywood. Made in 1961, *'Breakfast at Tiffany's'* was based on the novella written by Truman Capote. It produced a mesmeric performance by Audrey Hepburn.

The modern tale is transferred to London and

features the charismatic Ella van Houten and Harry, who is guilt ridden following the death of his wife. They meet in Regent Street in unusual circumstances. Their growing relationship parallels their search for a model of the Mexican general, Santa Anna, who burned 'The Alamo' to the ground.

The second publication, scheduled for April 2017, is **'Twelve Troubled Jurors'** with echoes of '*12 Angry Men*' which gave the film world one of Henry Fonda's greatest performances.

This will be followed by **'Forever on Thursdays'** which hints at the unforgettable British film '*Brief Encounter*'. The love affair between Celia Johnson and Trevor Howard remains an icon in film history.

-0-

Full details of the Novella Nostalgia series can be found at www.cityfiction.co.uk

ABOUT TONY DRURY

Tony is the author of five DCI Sarah Rudd City thrillers. In each, he draws upon his career as a London financier to expose the underworld of dark practices and shadowy characters. None, however, are able to withstand the bravery and incisive detection methods of one of the police force's bravest officers. Her juggling of career demands, husband, children and her own demons, make riveting reading.

He has now written two more novels which trace the early career of probationary police constable Sarah

Whitson. In 'On Scene and Dealing' she meets her future husband Nick. In 'Journey to the Crown' she has a devastating affair with Dr Martin Redding. The final chapter jumps ahead to sample her future life as a private detective.

Tony has created an innovative series as a novella writer. Reflecting iconic cinema classics, his first is 'Lunch with Harry', which is inspired by 'Breakfast at Tiffany's'. Others to follow include 'Twelve Troubled Jurors' (echoing '12 Angry Men') and 'Forever on Thursdays' (capturing the drama of 'Brief Encounter').

He writes short-stories wherein the net proceeds go to HEART UK – The Cholesterol Charity. He is an ambassador for the charity.

Aged seventy, Tony is a follower of the wisdom of Albert Einstein: "When a man stops learning, he starts dying." He lives in Bedford with his wife Judy. They value every trip down the M1 to Watford to be with Grandson Henry.

Connect with Tony online:
(e) tony@cityfiction.co.uk
(w) tonydrury.com
Twitter: mrtonydrury
Facebook: facebook.com/tony.drury.author
Goodreads: goodreads.com/TonyDrury